A HAPPY ENDING BOOK

the New Teacher

by Jane Carruth   illustrated by Tony Hutchings

MODERN PROMOTIONS/PUBLISHERS
A Division of Unisystems, Inc.
New York, New York 10022
Printed in Belgium

Tiggy always looked forward to school, as she liked her teacher very much. In the painting lesson, Tiggy painted a picture of the teacher. As soon as it was finished she showed it to her proudly. "It's very good," smiled her teacher.

One day the teacher told the class
that she was leaving. "You will have
a new teacher starting today," she
said. "Her name is Mrs. Prickles."
Tiggy was very upset. "I don't want
you to go," she cried.

Tiggy didn't want to eat her supper when she got home. "Our nice teacher has left," she told her mother. "Now we have a new teacher, called Mrs. Prickles. I don't like her."
"Now don't be silly," said Mommy. "You must try to like your new teacher."

But Tiggy had made up her mind not to like the
new teacher. She painted a messy picture, and was
so careless that she spilt the paint.

Some paint went on to Mrs. Prickles' apron. "Oh dear, she will be angry," thought Tiggy. But Mrs. Prickles said, "Never mind, it will wash off."

After the painting lesson Mrs. Prickles got out a
box of costumes. "We are going to put on
a play," she said, as she gave everyone a costume.
Tiggy wondered what she would get, but the
teacher didn't give her anything. "She must be angry
after all," Tiggy thought.

Then Mrs. Prickles gave Tiggy a lovely crown.
"Will you play the princess?" she smiled. "We will
need a new costume, as the old one is torn. You
will have to work hard—can you do it?"
"Oh, yes," said Tiggy happily. "I'll try hard."

"I'm going to be the princess in the school play!"
Tiggy told her mother. "Will you make me a dress,
and help me to learn my words?"

Tiggy's mother was very pleased. "Of course I will
help," she smiled, "and I will make you a beautiful
princess costume to wear."

The day before the play they dressed up in their costumes and practiced for the last time. Tiggy was very good, and Mrs. Prickles said that she looked like a real princess in the costume her mother had made for her.

"You have done very well," said the new teacher, "and I am very proud of you."

Everybody's parents came to see the play, and when at last the handsome prince rescued the lovely Princess Tiggy from the wicked pirates, they all clapped. Tiggy's mother and father clapped loudest of all, they were so proud of their little daughter.

After the play Tiggy took Mrs. Prickles to meet her
mother. "This is my new teacher, Mommy," she said.
"She's ever so nice!" And she smiled a big, happy
smile as they shook hands.
"I'm sure she is!" said Mommy.